THE GAMER

DIGITAL TERROR

by Shawn Pryor

illustrated by Francesca Ficorilli

Raintree is an imprint of Capstone Global Library Limited, a company
incorporated in England and Wales having its registered office at 264
Banbury Road, Oxford, OX2 7DY – Registered company number: 6695582

www.raintree.co.uk
myorders@raintree.co.uk

Designed by Hilary Wacholz
Original illustrations © Capstone Global Library Limited 2023
Originated by Capstone Global Library Ltd

978 1 3982 3977 7

British Library Cataloguing in Publication Data
A full catalogue record for this book is available from the British Library.

CONTENTS

You may believe that video games and apps are just harmless fun. But in these special places where we play, a hero works to protect us from the dangers that exist in those worlds . . .

Meet **THE GAMER**, defender of Earth and the digital realm!

REAL NAME: Tyler Morant

HERO NAME: The Gamer

AGE: 13

HERO TOOL: Gamer Activation
Device, which transforms
Tyler into the Gamer

ENEMY: Cynthia Cyber

MISSION: To defeat evil Cynthia Cyber
and her wicked digital monsters

CHAPTER 1

CYNTHIA'S SINISTER MONSTER

Cynthia Cyber is planning in her lab . . .

"I need to find a **monster**!" she says to herself.

Cynthia types on her computer. She is searching.

"There he is," she says. "**Terror Beast!** He'll **destroy** the city and the world."

Cynthia flips a few switches. A machine begins to hum and lights up her lab.

"Appear, Terror Beast!" Cynthia says.

With a **flash of light**, the Terror Beast appears.

The monster wears a spiked jacket, boots and clown make-up.

"You called for me?" asks the Terror Beast.

"I did, but you look **ridiculous**!" says Cynthia.

This angers the Terror Beast. Using his powers, he grows to twelve feet tall. He shows his **sharp teeth**. He shoots **laser beams** from his eyes.

Cynthia avoids the laser blast.
The **blast** makes a big hole in the wall.

BOOM!!

"I was wrong. You're **perfect**."
Cynthia smiles. "Destroy Crescent City!"

CHAPTER 2

TERROR STRIKES

Tyler is with his friends Kira and Jordan at the skate park.

Suddenly they hear a huge crashing sound.

Tyler looks in the distance.

A building **crumbles** in the city!
A weird fog covers the area.

"What's going on?" asks Kira.

A booming voice speaks. "I'll **destroy** this city! **Nothing** can stop me."

"Crescent City is in big trouble," says Tyler.

Tyler turns to his friends. "You two head home. Now!"

His friends hop on their skateboards. They leave.

Looking around the empty park, Tyler reveals the device on his wrist. He says, "**GAMER, TRANSFORM!**"

Tyler turns into **the Gamer**. He hops into his **TurboCraft** and races towards the centre of the city.

The Gamer enters the foggy area.
He activates the TurboCraft's scanning
device.

"I need to know **who or what** this
monster is," says the Gamer.

The TurboCraft responds. "Monster
identified. It is the Terror Beast."

"Terror Beast?" the Gamer says.
"Cynthia must've pulled him from
the *Monster-verse* game."

"I hate *Monster-verse*," he adds.
"The monsters in that game **scare** me!"

Suddenly a group of people scream out.

"Snakes! Snakes everywhere!"

"Get them off of us!"

"They're **crushing** us! Help us, please!"

CHAPTER 3

THE INVISIBLE ENEMY

"Please, help us! **Snakes!**" one person screams.

The Gamer looks at the people screaming and running around.

"There are no snakes," he tells them.

The people keep screaming.

"They must be having nightmares," the Gamer says. "The Terror Beast did this!"

The hero talks into his wrist device. "How can I help them?"

The device answers. "Terror Beast uses toxic fog to create **nightmares**. The fog must be removed."

That gives the hero an idea. "TurboCraft, **activate engine fan**," he says.

The engine fan **roars**, blowing the fog away from the city.

The nightmares end.

"What happened?" someone asks.

"It was a bad dream. I need to get you all out of here," says the Gamer.

The Gamer tells the TurboCraft, "**Activate transport carrier!**"

The TurboCraft turns itself into a large wagon.

The people get into the wagon.

"Get them to **safety**," the Gamer orders the TurboCraft.

The TurboCraft leaves. The air is quiet.

The Gamer looks around. "Where is the monster?" he wonders.

Suddenly the Terror Beast **grabs** the Gamer.

"Looking for me?" the monster asks.
He throws the Gamer through a building.

The building falls on the hero.

CHAPTER 4

FACING YOUR FEARS

The Terror Beast **grabs** the Gamer out of the rubble.

He **squeezes** the Gamer, making the hero's power suit crack!

"My toxic fog makes everyone fear the same thing. But my **VENOM** is worse," says the monster.

Venom **OOZES** from his hand. It covers the Gamer.

"No! Get this off me!" the Gamer screams.

The Terror Beast throws the hero to the ground.

"Your **worst fears** will take over your mind. Then you will fade away forever," the Terror Beast says, laughing.

The Gamer stands up. "No, I won't let them!"

But the Gamer is surrounded.

Monsters from video games he's too scared to play attack him.

He swings his energy sword! "Get away from me!" he yells. "**GET AWAY!**"

CHAPTER 5

A SWEATY BATTLE!

Aliens, gorillas and robotic spiders creep closer to the Gamer.

"Soon you'll be **finished**!" says the Terror Beast.

Suddenly the TurboCraft appears. It knocks the monster into a parked truck.

The Gamer **runs** from the aliens, gorillas and robotic spiders.

"Please, leave me alone, monsters!" he yells.

His wrist device starts to speak. **"Remove venom!"**

The Gamer's power suit starts to glow red. It gets very hot.

"What's going on?" the Gamer asks.

The Gamer starts sweating. **A lot!**
The monsters disappear.

"The venom! It's going away!"
the Gamer says.

Soon he is back to normal.

"The nightmares are **over**! You're
next, Terror Beast!" he shouts.

The monster picks up the parked truck.

He throws it at the Gamer.

The Gamer **slices** the truck in half with his sword.

He **super punches** the Terror Beast.

"TurboCraft, **activate power laser**!" the Gamer says.

The Gamer points at the Terror Beast.

"**FIRE!**" says the hero.

The TurboCraft shoots its **laser beam**.

The beam **zaps** the Terror Beast, destroying the monster.

"Crescent City is **saved**," says the hero. "At least for now . . ."

GLOSSARY

activate turn on or to become active

device piece of equipment that does a certain job

digital realm world created by video games, phone apps and the internet

identify tell what something is

reveal show clearly

ridiculous silly or unreasonable

terror something very scary

transform change one's appearance

venom poisonous liquid

TALK ABOUT IT

1. The TurboCraft was a big help to the Gamer. Explain how the TurboCraft helped the Gamer beat the Terror Beast.

2. Discuss why the Gamer became so scared in Chapter 4. How was he able to beat his fears?

WRITE ABOUT IT

1. If you had the Terror Beast's powers, what would you do with them? Write a paragraph explaining what you would do with those powers.

2. The book ends with the Gamer defeating the Terror Beast. But what about Crescent City? Who is going to clean things up? Write a story about how the city gets cleaned up.

THE AUTHOR

Shawn Pryor is the creator and co-author of the graphic novel mystery series Cash and Carrie, co-creator and author of the 2019 Glyph-nominated football/drama series Force and author of *Kentucky Kaiju* and *Diamond Double Play*, from Jake Maddox Sports Stories. In his free time, he enjoys reading, cooking, streaming music playlists, and talking about why Zack from *Mighty Morphin Power Rangers* is the greatest superhero of all time.

THE ILLUSTRATOR

Francesca Ficorilli was born and lives in Rome, Italy. Francesca knew that she wanted to be an artist when she was a child. She was encouraged by her love of animation and her mother's passion for fine arts. After earning a degree in animation, Francesca started working as a freelance animator and illustrator. She finds inspirations for her illustrations in every corner of the world.